DISNEY's

IT'S MAGIC!

STORIES FROM THE FILMS

BY TODD STRASSER
WITH POEMS BY RICHARD DUKE
ILLUSTRATED BY PHILIPPE HARCHY

Disney PRESS

NEW YORK

To Henriette Blinder, who makes magic moments every day
—T.S.

"Bibbidi-Bobbidi-Boo"
Words by Jerry Livingston.
Music by Mack David and Al Hoffman.
Copyright © 1948 by Walt Disney Music Company.
Copyright Renewed.
All Rights Reserved. Used by Permission.

First Edition
1 3 5 7 9 10 8 6 4 2

Library of Congress Catalog Card Number: 94-70814
ISBN 0-7868-3001-8/0-7868-5000-0 (lib. bdg.)

TABLE OF CONTENTS

SWEET DREAMS TO ALL

Two kings and a queen
And the knights standing guard—
Even the dogs are asleep in the yard!

The heralds are slumping,
They've lowered their flags.
Look at the horse and you'll see how he sags.

The cook in the kitchen,
The mouse nibbling cheese,
Now, Merryweather, put them to sleep, won't you please?

If they're all fast in slumber,
Then none will suppose
That we couldn't protect our sweet Briar Rose.

We just need more time
To undo this spell
And make the fair princess wake up and be well.

There's no time for pity—
Come, Fauna, stop weeping.
Just sprinkle that dust until everyone's sleeping!

THE PERFECT PARTY

For nearly sixteen years, Flora, Fauna, and Merryweather disguised themselves as peasants and raised Princess Aurora in secret. They even changed her name to Briar Rose to keep her safe from Maleficent's evil spell. Not even Briar Rose herself knew that she was a princess. If Maleficent had her way, the girl would have pricked her finger on the spindle of a spinning wheel and died long ago. But Maleficent had only until the princess's sixteenth birthday—today!—and so far she had been unable to find her.

Now it was time to tell Briar Rose the truth. Tonight the fairies would take her back to her real parents, the king and queen. But first they would surprise her with a birthday cake and a new dress worthy of a young princess.

Fauna sent Briar Rose out to pick berries in the forest. Then she thumbed through her cookbook for a cake recipe. "Ah! Here's one that sounds delicious!" she cried. "A fifteen-layer cake."

"But you've never cooked," Merryweather said.

"Oh, it's simple," Fauna replied, and began mixing the ingredients in a large wooden bowl. "All you do is follow the recipe."

Meanwhile, Flora, the eldest of the fairies, told Merryweather to step up on a stool and stay still while she draped cloth for the princess's dress around her.

"But you can't sew," Merryweather protested.

"Now, now, dear," said Flora, "I'm going to make a dress a princess can be proud of."

Despite the three fairies' best intentions, the preparations went poorly. With only minutes remaining before Briar Rose was to return from the forest, the fairies were in a panic. The dress Flora had sewn trapped poor Merryweather like a cocoon, and Fauna's tall birthday cake was tipping over and melting.

"Let me out of here!" Merryweather cried as she struggled against the fabric. "This dress looks awful!"

"That's because it's on you, dear," Flora shot back with a smile.

Meanwhile, Fauna propped up the falling cake with a broom. "Well, what do you think of it?" she asked.

"Why, it's a very unusual cake," Flora replied carefully.

"But it's dripping," observed Merryweather.

"It will be much stiffer after it's baked," explained Fauna.

Merryweather finally worked her way out of the dress. She couldn't believe the other two fairies were serious. The cake was collapsing, the dress was a disaster, and the cottage was a mess.

"I think we've had enough of this nonsense," she said in a huff as she stepped off the stool. "We ought to think of Rose and how she'll feel when she sees this. I'm going to get those wands."

Flora and Fauna glanced nervously at each other. In all the years they'd lived with the princess, they had not used their magic wands once. Any magical doings might have attracted the suspicions of Maleficent and revealed their hiding place. But with the princess's birthday almost over, it seemed impossible that the girl would now fall under the evil spell.

A moment later Merryweather came downstairs, carrying the wands. "Here they are, good as new."

"Careful, Merryweather," warned Flora as she took the three

magical sticks. "Quick! Lock the doors. Fauna, you close the windows. Plug up every cranny. We can't take any chances."

Merryweather and Fauna hurried about, sealing off every possible opening where the magic from their wands might seep out of the cottage. When they were done, they returned to Flora.

"You take care of the cake." Flora handed Fauna her wand, then turned to Merryweather. "And you clean the room, dear. I'll make the dress. Now, hurry."

"Come on, bucket, mop, and broom," muttered Merryweather, who would have preferred to make the dress. "Flora says clean up the room."

She waved her wand, and a shower of sparkles flew into the air and descended on the mop and broom. "Now, get to work," she ordered.

In an instant the mop and broom set to work sweeping and scrubbing the cottage by themselves.

Nearby, Fauna waved her wand over the cake ingredients, showering them with magic sparkles. "Eggs, flour, milk—just do like it says, here in the book. I'll put on the birthday candles."

In a flash the ingredients poured themselves into a bowl. A cloud of flour hung in the air as a wooden spoon beat and stirred the batter by itself. Moments later the whole bowl rose into the air and magically poured out a fully baked and wonderfully decorated cake.

Meanwhile, with a wave of *her* wand, Flora brought the pink fabric to life.

"And now to make a lovely dress," she said. "Fit to grace a fair princess."

The twinkling magic of her wand spread itself over scissors, needles, and thread. Suddenly they went to work as if guided by invisible hands, cutting, piecing, and sewing together the pink material. Soon a long, dazzling gown with a full skirt stood by itself in the center of the room for all to admire.

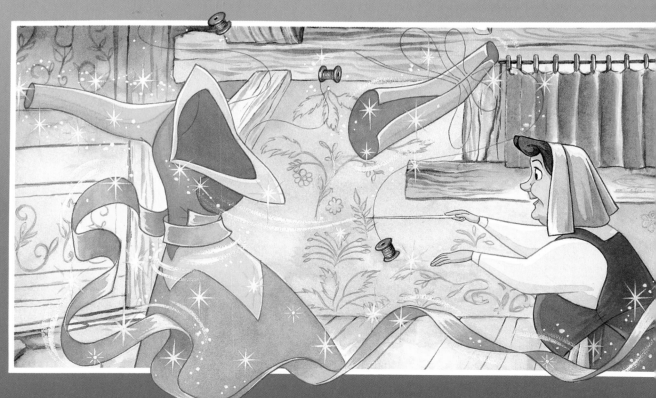

But Merryweather was far from pleased.

"Oh no, not pink!" she argued, still upset that she hadn't been allowed to make the dress. "Make it blue."

Aiming her wand, Merryweather sent a burst of blue glitter over the gown, instantly turning the fabric blue.

Flora looked up, startled. "Merryweather! Make it pink!" She waved *her* wand, flinging a shower of pink toward the blue dress. Once again the dress was pink, but not for long.

"Make it blue!" Merryweather cried, giving the dress another blast of blue.

"Pink!" Flora yelled, changing it back.

"Blue!"

"Pink!"

Soon bursts of blue and pink magic were rocketing around the cottage like bright glowing comets as Flora and Merryweather battled over the dress. Glittering sparkles burst and soared around the

two fairies. Their own clothes changed colors many times, and the dress became a splotchy mixture of hues.

"Oh, now look what you've done!" Flora cried angrily.

"*Shhh.*" Fauna held a finger to her lips. "Listen!"

They could hear footsteps outside.

"It's the princess!" Merryweather whispered.

"She's back," hissed Flora. "Enough of this foolishness."

Merryweather quickly finished cleaning the cottage while Fauna lit the candles on the cake.

"Pink!" Flora turned the dress pink for the last time. "Now hide, quick!" she whispered hoarsely.

She and Fauna hurried to hide on the stairs. Suddenly left alone, Merryweather saw her chance. "Blue!" she cried gleefully, and aimed her wand at the dress. A final cloud of magic burst from the tip of her wand and swirled around the dress, turning it blue.

Briar Rose was coming up the path toward the cottage. Merryweather scurried to the stairs and hid with the others. There was no time for Flora to change the color of the dress back to pink again.

"Good gracious!" Flora gasped, pointing at the mop, which was still swabbing the floor by itself. "Who left the mop running?"

"Stop, mop!" Merryweather ordered with a wave of her wand, and the mop clattered to the floor.

A moment later Briar Rose pushed open the door and stepped in. "Aunt Flora, Fauna, Merryweather," she called. "Where is every—"

Her voice trailed off as her eyes fell on the beautiful dress and the wonderful cake. Just then the three good fairies hopped out from their hiding place.

"Surprise!" they shouted. "Happy birthday!"

The princess's jaw dropped, and she clasped her hands together. "Oh, you darlings! This is the happiest day of my life!"

"And the most *magical*!" whispered Fauna to the other fairies with a wink.

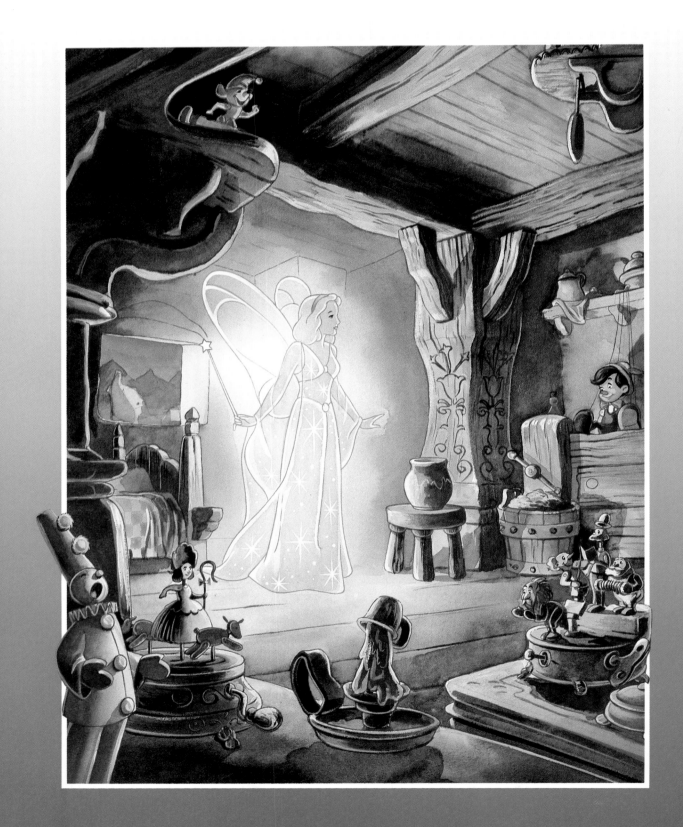

LITTLE PUPPET MADE OF PINE

Tonight as I was looking down
Upon a snowy little town

I saw, though all was dark and still,
An old man at his windowsill.

A wood-carver he seemed to be
For all around him I could see

The wondrous things he'd made himself
On every table, every shelf:

A rocking horse, a music box,
A dozen ticking wooden clocks.

And leaning there against the wall,
The most remarkable of all,

A wooden boy with such appeal
I almost thought that he was real.

And then I knew what I could do
To make Geppetto's wish come true.

I'd take this charming wooden toy
And change him to a living boy:

Little puppet made of pine,
Wake! The gift of life is thine!

STAR LIGHT, STAR BRIGHT

From her perch high in the night sky, the Blue Fairy gazed down at the quaint little town where Geppetto the wood-carver lived. It was late, and most of the houses were dark. But Geppetto's window was open, and the kindly old man was kneeling by it in his nightclothes, making a wish.

Star light, star bright,
First star I see tonight,
I wish I may, I wish I might
Have the wish I make tonight!

The Blue Fairy listened as Geppetto asked that his newest creation, the puppet he called Pinocchio, might become a real boy. The fairy knew that Geppetto had never had a son. He was a good man who deserved to have his wish come true. And so she made up her mind to help him.

Moments later, as Geppetto lay fast asleep in his bed, the star he had wished upon began to move through the sky, growing larger and shining more brightly as it drew closer to the earth. Now a large ball of light, it floated through the open window and entered the small room where the wood-carver both lived and worked, illuminating the shelves of beautifully carved clocks and playful music boxes he had fashioned out of wood.

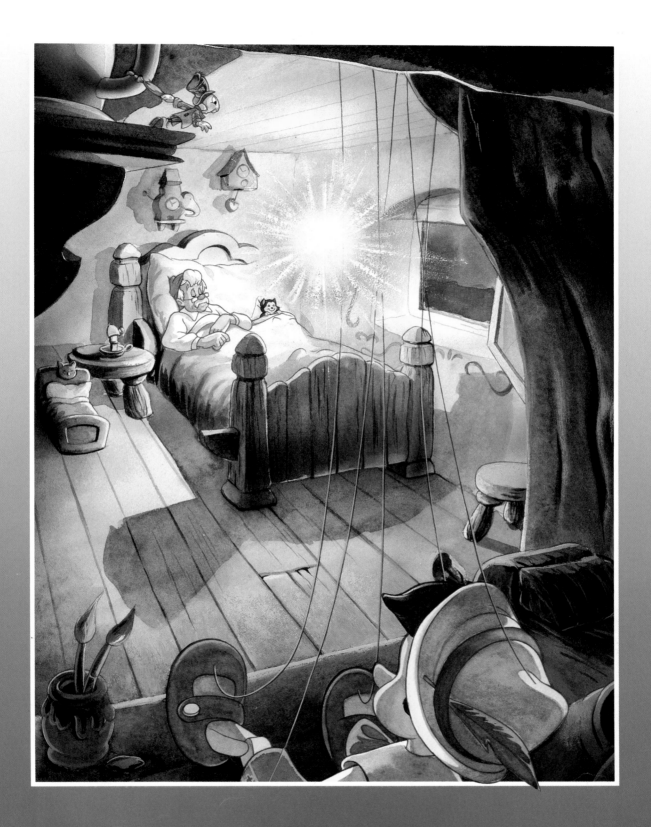

Geppetto lay in his bed with his cat, Figaro, unaware of the celestial presence just a few feet away. As it settled to the floor, the bright light magically changed into a beautiful woman. Her blond hair shone against her sparkling blue dress, and a pair of delicate wings shimmered on her back. A gleaming aura of light radiated around her. Carrying a wand with a gold star at its tip, she stepped up to the bed and stood over the snoring wood-carver.

"Good Geppetto," she said softly, "you have given so much happiness to others. Now you deserve to have *your* wish come true."

She turned to the wooden puppet, which Geppetto had propped up on a bench. As the Blue Fairy drew close, Pinocchio's painted face reflected the light that filled the room.

"Little puppet made of pine, wake!" the Blue Fairy whispered. The gold star at the tip of her wand began to glow, and she touched it to the puppet's head. "The gift of life is thine!"

The same glow that surrounded the Blue Fairy now encircled the lifeless puppet. Though Pinocchio was still made of wood, glue, and paint, his strings suddenly vanished. The little puppet blinked and rubbed his eyes. He stared around the room with an astonished look and opened and closed his hands.

"I can move!" he gasped.

Surprised by the sound of his own voice, Pinocchio momentarily clapped his hands over his mouth, then let go.

"I can talk!" he cried with childish delight.

The Blue Fairy couldn't help but laugh.

Pinocchio pushed himself up on his feet. "I can walk!" But the words were hardly out of his mouth when he lost his balance and toppled backward.

"Yes, Pinocchio," the Blue Fairy said. "I have given you life."

The puppet boy looked up at her with shy, innocent eyes. "Why?" he asked.

"Because tonight Geppetto wished for a real boy," she replied.

"Am I a *real* boy?" Pinocchio asked in wonder.

"Well, not yet, Pinocchio," the Blue Fairy answered. "To make Geppetto's wish come true will be entirely up to you."

"Up to *me*?" Pinocchio repeated uncertainly.

"You must prove yourself brave, truthful, and unselfish, and some-day you will be a *real* boy," she assured him.

Pinocchio clapped his hands together happily. "A real boy!"

"But first you must learn to choose between right and wrong," the Blue Fairy cautioned.

"Right and wrong?" Pinocchio looked at his right hand and then at his left. "But how will I know?"

"Your conscience will tell you."

"Oh." Pinocchio nodded. "What's a conscience?"

19

Just then a small cricket wearing tattered clothes floated down from a shelf, using his umbrella as a parachute. Bathed in the Blue Fairy's glowing light, he landed on Geppetto's workbench and looked up at Pinocchio.

"What's a conscience?" the cricket repeated. "I'll tell you. A conscience is that small voice inside that people don't listen to."

Hooking a matchbox with his umbrella, the cricket pulled it over and stepped up on it as he started to deliver a lecture. "That's just the trouble with the world today," he glowered. "You see—"

"Are *you* my conscience?" Pinocchio cut in.

"Who, me?" The cricket was caught off guard.

The Blue Fairy leaned close to him and smiled. "Would you like to be Pinocchio's conscience?"

"Well . . . uh . . . ," he stammered and blushed, and pulled the collar of his tattered shirt away from his neck. Then he nodded. "Well, sure."

"Very well." The Blue Fairy was pleased that Pinocchio would have a friend to guide him, for the puppet boy would soon learn that the world outside was filled with temptations.

"What is your name?" she asked.

"Huh? Oh, uh, Cricket's the name." He took off his torn top hat and bowed. "Jiminy Cricket."

The Blue Fairy smiled. "Kneel, Mr. Cricket."

"Huh? No tricks now," Jiminy said as he kneeled and closed his eyes.

Once again the star at the end of her wand began to glow. The Blue Fairy waved the wand, shrouding Jiminy in bright, magical light. "I dub you Pinocchio's conscience," she said. "Keeper of the knowledge of right and wrong. Counselor in moments of temptation. Guide along the straight and narrow path. . . . Arise, Sir Jiminy Cricket!"

As Jiminy rose, the magic light around him cleared. The cricket was startled to discover that his tattered clothes had disappeared. He now wore a brand-new suit of the highest quality, with a shiny top hat and a gold-tipped umbrella.

"Well, ho, ho, ho!" Jiminy proudly spun in a circle, admiring himself. "Say, that's pretty swell. Thanks, but don't I get a badge or something?"

"Well, we'll see," the Blue Fairy replied in an amused voice.

"You mean, maybe I will?" Jiminy asked eagerly. Filled with excitement, he jumped up in the air and clapped his hands together. "Can you make it a gold one?"

"Maybe," the Blue Fairy replied with a smile. It was time for her to go, and she turned her attention to Pinocchio for one last word of advice. "Now, remember, be a good boy. And always let your conscience be your guide."

Pinocchio and Jiminy watched with astonishment as the Blue Fairy backed away slowly and disappeared in a cloud of bright light, returning once again to her place among the stars.

21

MERLIN'S MAGIC

To grant your wish to be a fish
Or vanish in thin air

To stack your plates when you are late
And haven't time to spare

To change your shape into an ape,
A turtle, snake, or bear

To give you wings and talk of things
To make you more aware

For evil foes may give you blows
And tell you to beware

When you're at court, be careful, Wart,
To handle things with care

I'll do my part and use my art
To help in this affair.

BRAINS OVER BRAWN

One afternoon the wizard Merlin took Wart for a walk along the castle moat. The boy's head was filled with dreams of riding white stallions and slaying fierce dragons, but Merlin was more interested in teaching Wart how to use his greatest strengths—his intelligence and his imagination.

"Now, lad," he began, "when I said that I could swim like a fish, I meant *as* a fish."

"You mean, you can really turn yourself into a fish?" Wart asked, looking up at him.

"Well, of course," Merlin replied. "After all, I happen to be a wizard."

"Could you turn *me* into a fish?"

"Well, do you have any imagination?" the wizard asked. "Can you imagine yourself as a fish?"

"Oh, that's easy," said the boy. "I've done it lots of times."

"Very good then," Merlin said, for it occurred to him that it might be helpful to see how the boy coped with being an altogether different creature. Of course, it would take some complicated magic, but that shouldn't be a problem. Merlin raised the old wooden cane that doubled as his wand.

"Um . . . Uh . . . Oh drat!" Unable to recall the precise formula, the wizard pointed his cane upward and poked Archimedes the owl,

who was perched on his hat. "Archimedes, what is that fish formula?"

With the help of the owl, Merlin chanted the spell: *"Aquarius, aquaticus, aqualitis, qwum . . . Aqua-digi-tonium!"*

A spiral of magic dust engulfed Wart, followed by a loud *poof!* and a cloud of smoke. Where the boy had just stood, a small orange fish now flopped on the grass.

"Merlin!" Wart cried. "Am I a fish?"

Merlin quickly kneeled down and tried to grab the slippery little fellow, but Wart kept popping out of the old Wizard's hands. "Yes, yes, you're a fish. But if you don't stop flippity-flopping around and get in the water, you won't last long."

On his next try Merlin almost got him, but the small fish tumbled into the Wizard's long white beard and disappeared. Several anxious moments passed before Merlin actually got hold of Wart and dropped him into the moat.

"Now stay there," Merlin ordered. "I'll be right with you."

Using the same magic formula, the wizard transformed himself into a fish and plopped down into the moat to look around for his young student. All he found was a small orange tail sticking out of the muddy bottom.

"So, you thought you could take off like a shot, did you?" Merlin asked with a chuckle as he pulled the mud-covered fish out. Wart floated upward as the mud fell away.

"Well, I *am* a fish, aren't I?" the boy asked as he rolled helplessly in the water.

"You merely *look* like a fish," Merlin corrected him. "That doesn't mean you can swim like one. You don't have the instinct, so you'll have to use your brain for a change."

Merlin swam toward Wart, who was still struggling in his new, watery environment.

"Every flick of a fin creates movement," the wizard lectured. "So we'll start with your tail fin."

Fin by fin, Merlin taught Wart how to move in the water. Soon the two of them were swimming along quite gaily. Then, suddenly, a bullfrog grabbed Wart by the tail.

"Let go, let go!" Wart shouted, trying to get free. The bullfrog let go, and the little fish was catapulted forward as if from a slingshot. "Oh, you big bug-eyed bully!" he shouted angrily.

"Here, here, boy," Merlin said. "There's no sense going around insulting bullfrogs. A fish has plenty of other problems without that. The water world has its forests and jungles, too. It has its tigers and wolves. You see, my boy, that's nature's way. The strong ones prey upon the weak. It's also true in human life. The strong will try to conquer you."

"They will?" Wart asked.

"Yes," the wizard nodded. "That's what you must expect unless you use your head. It's brains versus brawn and weak versus strong, and that's what makes—"

"Help!" Wart shouted.

Merlin was startled to see the little fish race past, pursued by a monstrous pike with long, sharp teeth.

"Gee-hosa-fat!" Merlin gasped, grabbing the pike's tail to stop him from gobbling up Wart. The pike angrily shook his tail loose, sending the wizard spinning into a rusty knight's helmet at the bottom of the moat.

Clank! The helmet's visor snapped shut, trapping Merlin inside. Meanwhile, the pike raced after Wart.

"Quick, Merlin!" the little fish shouted. "Use your magic!"

"No, no, you're on your own, lad," Merlin called back. "Now's your chance to prove my point."

"What point?" Wart gasped in terror as he swam around wildly.

"That he's the brawn and you're the brain," Merlin replied. "Don't panic. Use your head. Outsmart the brute."

Merlin watched as Wart deftly led the pike through a link in a heavy chain. The little fish fit through easily, but the much larger pike got stuck.

"Smart move, lad!" Merlin cheered. "That's using the old intellect! We don't always have to rely on magic!"

But the pike shook free and came after Wart again. The little fish looked around for something to defend himself with and spied a broken arrow on the moat's bottom. He quickly swam down and picked it up, but the pike had disappeared. Wart swam around nervously, looking for him.

Suddenly the pike appeared behind Wart. The little fish quickly jammed the arrow into the pike's mouth, wedging it open.

"Bravo, boy! Great strategy!" Merlin cheered as Wart escaped once again.

"Is the lesson about over?" the boy asked hopefully from his hiding place behind the helmet.

"Did you get the point?" Merlin asked.

"Yes," Wart gasped. "Brains over brawn!"

"Okay then," Merlin said. It was time to cast a spell before anything really awful happened. "I'll fix the brute. *Higgledy-piggledy* . . . What in blazes?"

He tried to recite the magic chant that would free him from the old helmet, but the words got jumbled, and this time Archimedes wasn't there to help. Meanwhile, the pike snapped the broken arrow in half and started after Wart again, now angrier than before.

"*Merlin!*" poor Wart cried as the pike raced after him. A wild chase followed, and Wart surely would have been eaten had it not been for Archimedes, who, following the action from above, swooped down and plucked the little fish from the water just in time. Merlin finally chanted the right words to turn himself back into his human form. Moments later he swam to the surface, climbed out of the moat, flung off the helmet, and grabbed his cane.

"What in thunder is a monster like that doing in a moat?" he shouted, waving his cane and storming back toward the water. "By George, I'll . . . I'll turn him into a minnow!"

"Merlin!" a voice shouted.

The sopping-wet wizard spun around and found Wart flopping on the grass behind him. "Oh, there you are! *Snick, snack, snorum!*"

With a flick of the cane the spell was broken, and Wart turned back into a boy again.

"How in the world did you ever get out of that mess?" Merlin asked.

"Archimedes saved me," Wart explained.

Merlin turned and found the owl lying upside down against a tree, with water spouting out of his beak.

"Well, what do you know about that?" The wizard couldn't help chuckling. He was glad that the day's lesson had ended successfully. True, it had been a bit more exciting than he'd anticipated, but the boy had learned a lot about brains versus brawn. And, after all, all was well that ended well.

As they headed back toward the castle, Merlin thought about the next day's lesson. Perhaps he would explain to Wart that the world was round, not flat. Or maybe he would show Wart an airplane— even though man wouldn't actually invent one for hundreds of years. With the aid of the wizard's magic, the boy was sure to learn a lot.

VISITORS, AT LAST!

Now you see me—
      now you don't!
If you look around,
      you won't,
Because I'm all rolled up snug.
      Hey, monkey! It's me—the rug!

Now you see me
      on the ground.
Soon I'll be following
      you around.
There's lots of treasure deep inside—
      hey, monkey—want to go for a ride?

A STROKE OF GENIE-US!

Aladdin and his monkey, Abu, were trapped in the Cave of Wonders. Not even the magic carpet could get them out now. Aladdin stared down at the dented old lamp he had been sent to retrieve.

"It looks like such a beat-up, worthless piece of junk," he muttered hopelessly. "Wait, I think there's something written here, but it's hard to make out."

Aladdin rubbed the lamp with his sleeve. Suddenly the lamp started to glow! Colorful smoke spewed out of the spout and filled the cave, whirling crazily into a huge blue cloud. As the boy and the monkey watched, amazed, the cloud grew arms, a chest, a head, and a wild-eyed face with a curling black beard.

"Oy!" the genie cried, grabbing his head with his hands and twisting it all the way around. "Ten thousand years in a lamp will give you *such* a crick in the neck!"

The genie stretched his arms. "Wow! Does it feel good to be outta there! I'm telling you. Nice to be back. So what's your name, kid?" he asked, now noticing the boy and the monkey.

"Uh . . . Aladdin."

"Hello, Aladdin, nice to have you on the show!" the genie said jokingly. "Can we call you Al? Or maybe just Din? Or how about Laddie?" The genie magically transformed into a giant blue Scottie dog and whistled, "Here, Laddie!"

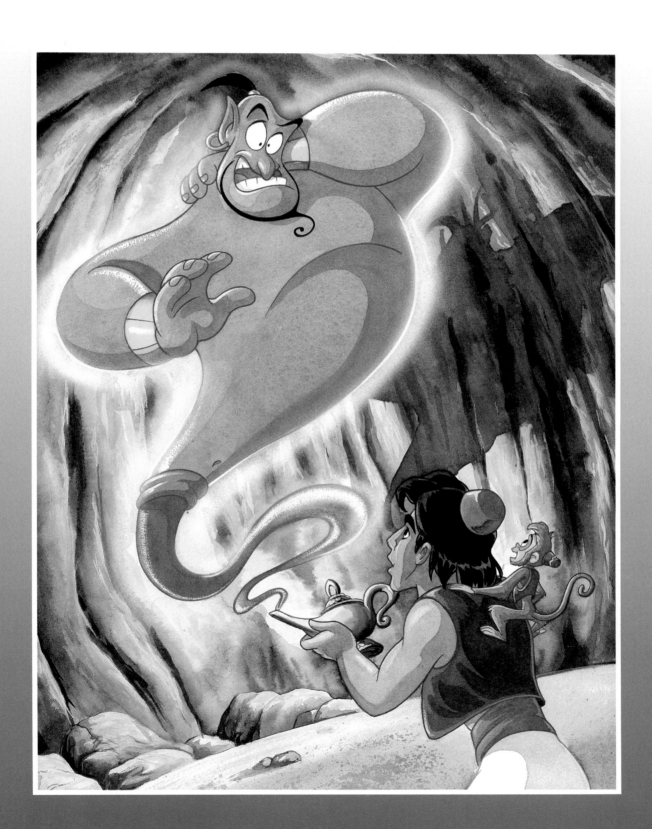

Aladdin couldn't believe what he was seeing. He shook his head and turned to the carpet. "I must have hit my head harder than I thought."

The genie suddenly returned to his original form. "Say, Aladdin, you're a lot smaller than my last master."

"I'm your *master*?" Aladdin gasped.

"That's right. And I am your genie, here for your wish fulfillment. You get three wishes—and *ix-nay* on wishing for more wishes."

"Any three I want?" Aladdin asked, wide-eyed.

"Actually, there are a few limitations," the genie replied. "One, I can't kill anybody, so don't ask. Two, I can't make anyone fall in love with anyone else. Three, I can't bring people back from the dead. Other than that, you got it!"

To the genie's surprise, the boy didn't seem impressed. "Limitations? Some all-powerful genie you are." Aladdin turned to Abu and, with a sly glance, said, "He probably can't even get us out of this cave. Looks like *we're* gonna have to find our own way out."

Aladdin started to walk away, followed by Abu and the carpet. The genie was shocked. In all his years he'd never had a master doubt him.

"Excuse me!" he huffed. "Did you rub my lamp? Did you bring me here? And all of a sudden you're walkin' out? I don't think so. You're getting your wishes, so *sit down*!"

The genie scooped up Aladdin and Abu and plunked them down on the magic carpet. He'd show them a thing or two. He raised his hand over his head and began to spin around like a giant blue top. A huge gust of funneling wind roared through the cave, and a thunderous *boom!* resounded above them as the cavern's ceiling cracked open. Rocks and sand poured down through long shafts of sunlight. Aladdin and Abu held tight as the carpet spun upward, lifting them out of the cave and into the morning desert air.

The genie couldn't help laughing when he saw the delighted looks on their faces. Surely they didn't doubt him *now*.

The carpet settled down in a lush oasis nearby, and Aladdin and Abu got off.

"Well, how about that?" the genie asked proudly.

"Oh, you sure showed me," Aladdin replied. "Now, about my three wishes. . . ."

The genie was certain he'd heard wrong. "Three? You're down by one, boy."

"No," Aladdin said with a mischievous smile. "I never actually *wished* to get out of the cave. You did that on your own."

The genie felt his jaw go slack. The boy was right. He'd been cleverly tricked. "Okay, kid, you got me this time, but that's it. No more freebies."

Aladdin paced about, trying to think. "Hmmm . . . three wishes . . . Well, what would *you* wish for?"

"Me?" the genie asked, startled. No other master had ever asked him that. "Well, in my case, it's easy," the genie said. "I'd wish for freedom."

"You're a prisoner?" Aladdin asked with a puzzled look.

The genie shrugged. "That's what being a genie's all about, kid. Phenomenal cosmic powers, itty-bitty living space."

To prove his point, the genie stuffed his giant form back into the small brass lamp. Aladdin peered in. The genie was squeezed in so tightly he couldn't move.

"That's terrible," Aladdin said. He thought for a moment. "I'll set you free," he said. The genie gave him a doubtful look. "Really, I promise. After I make my first two wishes, I'll use my third to set you free."

"Well, here's hoping," the genie said, not sure whether to believe the boy. "Anyway, let's make some magic. What is it *you* want most?"

"Well," Aladdin said. "There's this girl—"

"Wrong! I can't make anyone fall in love, remember?"

"But Genie, she's smart and fun and beautiful."

The genie turned to Abu and winked. *"C'est l'amour,"* he gushed romantically.

"But she's a princess," Aladdin said sadly. "To even have a chance, I'd have to be . . ." Aladdin suddenly stared up at the genie as if he'd had a brainstorm. "Hey, can you make me a prince?"

"Is this an *official* wish?" the genie asked, not wanting to be tricked again. "Say the magic words."

"Genie, I wish for you to make me a prince!"

"All right!" the genie cried. He circled Aladdin like a clothing designer with a critical eye. Then, with a sweeping gesture, the genie cast a magic spell. The air around Aladdin glimmered and twinkled as his ragged street clothes were replaced with robes of the finest silk and a turban with a dazzling jewel. Aladdin admired himself in the mirror the genie had conveniently conjured up.

"Ooh, I like it!" the genie shouted. But there was something missing. The genie realized what it was. Princes didn't get around

on foot. This prince needed transportation. The genie snapped his fingers at Abu. The reluctant monkey rose into the air and spun around so fast he became a blur.

When Abu stopped spinning—and much to his dismay—he'd been transformed into a camel.

"No, not enough," the dissatisfied genie said. He snapped his fingers, and Abu began to spin again, kicking up sand and dust.

The next thing Abu knew, he was a stallion.

"Still not enough," the genie said with a shake of his head. He snapped his fingers, and Abu spun once more. This time the whirling blur grew larger. Now Abu was an elephant!

"Talk about trunk space!" The genie laughed gleefully and turned to Aladdin. "Check this guy out! He's got the outfit. He's got the elephant. Hang on to your turban, kid. We're gonna make you a star!"

The genie settled back into the lamp, which Aladdin tucked under his new turban. Now the prince who had been a beggar and the elephant who'd been a monkey were whisked away on the magic carpet—straight to Agrabah!

SWEPT AWAY

If I were the sorcerer,
       what spell would I cast?
If I had his magic,
       how long would it last?
If I had his hat—
       would I still fill the vat?

Perhaps I would create
       a magical broom,
Then sit back and watch
       while it cleaned the room.
If I had my way,
       I would conjure all day!

     I'd aspire
     To make fire.

     I wonder . . .
     Could I make thunder?

     I'd try
     A butterfly—

     Why wouldn't I?

I guess I should stop
       and finish my work.
I'm really no more than
       a sorcerer's clerk.
But if I had his hat . . .
       I'd be greater than that!

WATERY WIZARDRY

As the Sorcerer's apprentice reached the stone well, he paused to rest his weary arms and wipe his brow. Lugging heavy buckets of water up and down the castle steps wasn't easy. Mickey had been an apprentice for many months, yet all the Sorcerer would let him do was tidy up the chamber and carry the day's water from the fountain to the well. Lately the young apprentice had begun to grow impatient to try the skills of his master. He wanted to perform grand magic just like the Sorcerer.

A glowing light caught his attention, and he turned to watch the bearded Sorcerer conjure smoke from a magic skull. Raising his arms again and again, the Sorcerer urged the smoke to rise above him and take the form of a huge, frightening red bat with shining yellow eyes. Mickey would have been terrified had he not seen this before. Then, as if to further demonstrate his magical skills, the Sorcerer transformed the bat into a giant butterfly of many beautiful colors.

The apprentice watched in awe. How he yearned to perform magic instead of dragging heavy buckets of water up the stairs every night!

Weary from his work, the Sorcerer waved his arms, and the butterfly dissolved into a shower of colorful particles that vanished with a powerful burst of light. Then the Sorcerer yawned, removed his magic hat, and left the room.

The apprentice caught his breath. Never before had his master

left the hat behind. As soon as the Sorcerer disappeared up the stairs, Mickey rushed to the table and tried the hat on. Now, at last, he would finally have the chance to perform magic.

Spying a broom leaning against the wall, Mickey pushed up his sleeves and flung his arms out toward it. In response, the broom began to flicker and glow. Again and again the apprentice reached toward it, straining to cast the spell until the broom glowed bright green and stood up.

Filled with excitement, Mickey beckoned the broom toward him, then made it stop between the two empty water buckets. The apprentice snapped his fingers and pointed to a bucket.

The broom grew an arm.

Mickey snapped his fingers again and the broom grew a second arm.

There! He could do it! He could make magic!

Flushed with success, he ordered the broom to pick up the buckets and follow him out of the room and up the stairs to the courtyard. There he showed the broom how to scoop buckets of water out of the fountain.

Moments later, lugging the heavy buckets, the broom followed the delighted apprentice back inside. Mickey skipped merrily down the steps. Not only had he used magic, but he no longer had to carry water.

With great pleasure he watched the broom empty the buckets into the well and make another trip to the fountain. This magic business is a snap, Mickey told himself, brimming with confidence. Then he settled down into the Sorcerer's chair, put his feet up on the Sorcerer's table, and promptly fell asleep.

He dreamed of performing even greater magic, of climbing to the top of a tall peak and commanding the stars to whirl around him like glowing comets before smashing together in a symphony of spectacular lights. He dreamed of calling on the sea to mount great crashing waves and of ordering huge clouds to thunder and crackle with lightning at a mere flick of his finger. He smiled and sighed as the sky boomed and the giant waves, one after another, crashed against his rocky perch. Now he was the greatest sorcerer on earth, controlling the sky and the seas and the heavens above.

But, alas, it was only a dream. . . .

Ker-splash!

Mickey awoke to find himself drenched. The Sorcerer's table and chair were floating away. Utterly confused, Mickey spun around and saw that the well was overflowing into the Sorcerer's chamber and the broom had gone to refill the buckets yet again. It had to be stopped before it flooded the entire castle.

With arms outstretched, Mickey splashed through the waist-deep water to the bottom of the steps. As the broom descended with two more buckets, the apprentice tried to undo the magic spell, but the words wouldn't come out right. The determined broom knocked him down and marched right past.

Mickey jumped up and tried to pull the buckets away but only managed to get himself thrown into the well. Meanwhile, the broom raced back up the stairs. Looking around in desperation, the apprentice saw an ax hanging on the wall. He grabbed it and raced outside.

Crack! Crack! Crack! The broom and the buckets were smashed into a thousand splinters.

The castle became quiet. Weary from all the excitement, Mickey trudged back toward the Sorcerer's chamber and closed the door behind him. He'd had a close call, but with any luck the extra water would drain away by morning and the Sorcerer would never suspect what had happened.

Relieved, Mickey started toward his room. Now he could truly rest. *Drip . . . splash . . . drip . . .* He heard a sound and stared at the

door. *No, it couldn't be!* he thought. *Drip . . . splash . . . drip . . .* Yanking the door open, he beheld a horrible sight: A thousand brooms were now marching down the steps toward him. And each one carried two buckets *full* of water.

Slamming the door shut, the apprentice pressed himself against it. If only he knew how to undo the spell. He pushed against the door as hard as he could, but it was no use. The door flew open, knocking him to the floor, and a thousand brooms began to trample over him as they carried their buckets to the well.

Splash . . . splash . . . splash! They emptied two thousand buckets and went back for more. The water rose and rose until the helpless apprentice could no longer feel the floor beneath him. All the Sorcerer's belongings, large and small, swirled around in the water. Mickey watched in horror as beakers and flasks—even the Sorcerer's great big book of spells—floated past. No sooner had he flung himself onto the soaked book than he was swept into a mighty whirlpool. Around and around he spun, unable to escape certain doom!

Oh, how he regretted using magic!

Suddenly the whirlpool stopped, and the water quickly drained away. The next thing he knew, the startled apprentice found himself lying on the wet floor, next to a broom and two buckets.

The spell had been broken! But how? he wondered.

Looking up, he saw the answer in the glowering face of his master. The Sorcerer scowled, and the apprentice meekly rose to his feet and removed the magic hat. The Sorcerer grabbed it away angrily. Mickey offered him the broom, and the Sorcerer took that, too. Finally, Mickey picked up his wooden buckets to show the Sorcerer that he knew what his real job was.

As the apprentice started to tiptoe away, a slight smile creased the Sorcerer's lips. His apprentice had learned a valuable lesson: Even the simplest magic is dangerous in unskilled hands.

WHAT'S A FAIRY GODMOTHER TO DO?

Oh my goodness . . . where's my wand?
Where's a pumpkin? I'll need mice.
She'll have to get there in a coach—
Of course, she'll need a dress that's nice.

Am I too late? Are they all at the palace?
She doesn't have much time.
I must remember to tell her
About that midnight chime.

Poor Cinderella, she's in tears,
And I am in a flurry—
But I'll get her to the ball tonight.
Oh, where *is* my wand—I must hurry!

BIBBIDI-BOBBIDI-BOO

It's just no use," Cinderella sobbed, with tears running down her face. "No use at all."

Her ugly stepsisters had torn her beautiful dress to shreds. Now she had no hope of attending the king's ball. It seemed that she would be a prisoner in that house and a slave to her heartless stepmother and stepsisters forever.

"I can't believe . . . not anymore," Cinderella cried hopelessly. "There's nothing left to believe in."

But even as Cinderella spoke those sad words, the air around her gleamed with tiny flecks of light, and her fairy godmother, a plump, sweet-looking woman wearing a blue hooded shawl, suddenly appeared.

"Nothing, my dear?" the woman asked gently. "Oh, now, you don't really mean that."

"I do!" Cinderella insisted without realizing who had spoken to her.

"Nonsense, child," her fairy godmother said. "If you'd lost all your faith, I wouldn't be here. And here I am."

Cinderella looked up, puzzled. Her fairy godmother wasn't a bit surprised by her reaction. After all, it wasn't every day that a girl met her fairy godmother. She helped Cinderella to her feet.

"Come now," she said. "Dry those tears. You can't go to the ball looking like that."

"The ball?" Cinderella was perplexed. "But I'm not—"

"Of course you are," said the fairy as she pushed up her sleeves. "But we'll have to hurry, because even miracles take a little time."

"Miracles?" Cinderella repeated.

"Watch." The fairy reached for her wand, then suddenly realized she didn't have it. "What in the world did I do with that magic wand?"

"Magic wand?" Cinderella gasped. "Then you must be—"

"Your fairy godmother," the fairy said, as if it were obvious. She searched around the bench. "Now, where in the world. . . ? Oh, I forgot! I put it away."

She straightened up and made the wand appear out of thin air. Cinderella's eyes went wide.

"Now, let's see," the fairy said. "I'd say the first thing you need is a pumpkin."

Again Cinderella was caught by surprise. "A pumpkin?"

"*Salaga-doola, menchicka-boola,*" the fairy chanted, and waved her wand. "*Bibbidi-bobbidi-boo.*"

Cinderella watched in amazement as a stream of twinkling magic left the tip of the wand and traveled to a pumpkin lying in a nearby field. The magic swirled and sparkled around the pumpkin. Suddenly it began to glow—and grow! Winding tendrils formed beautiful white wheels as the pumpkin miraculously transformed into a dazzling white-and-gold carriage with a plush pink interior.

"It's beautiful," Cinderella cried.

"Isn't it?" the fairy godmother replied, rather pleased with her work. "Now, with a fancy coach like that, we'll simply have to have some . . . mice!"

"Mice?"

"Oh, this really is perfect." The fairy waved her wand at some mice that had collected near the coach. "Why, we'll have a coach and four when we're through. Just a wave of my wand, and . . . *bibbidi-bobbidi-boo!*"

Once again the glittering magic burst from her wand and settled like a delicate cloud around the mice. Cinderella watched in awe as the little animals grew into four magnificent white stallions with flowing manes and golden stirrups.

In short order Cinderella's fairy godmother transformed the family horse into a handsome coachman, and the family hound, Bruno, into a gallant footman.

"Now, hop in, my dear," she said to Cinderella. "We can't waste time."

"But, uh. . . ," the young girl hesitated.

"Oh, now, now, don't try to thank me," her fairy godmother said.

"Oh, I wasn't," Cinderella said, and then caught herself. "I mean, I do. But, uh, don't you think my dress. . . ?"

"Oh, it's lovely, dear, just—" The fairy suddenly noticed Cinderella's torn dress. "Good heavens, child, you can't go in that!"

Cinderella sighed with relief as her fairy godmother began to circle her. "Let's see, dear," she mumbled. "Your size and the shade of your eyes . . . hmmm . . . Something simple—but elegant, too. Just leave it to me."

She waved her magic wand, and Cinderella was engulfed in a swirling, gleaming light as her torn dress turned into a dazzling blue gown.

"Oh, it's beautiful!" the young girl gasped. She spun toward the footman, who was holding open the door to the carriage. "Did you ever see such a beautiful dress? And look, glass slippers."

Cinderella showed the footman her slippers, then twirled back to her fairy godmother. "It's like a dream," she cried happily. "A wonderful dream come true!"

The fairy godmother was glad that Cinderella was so happy, but

she had to remember to tell her something. "Yes, my child, but like all dreams, this one can't last forever. You'll have only until midnight—"

"Midnight?" Cinderella looked up from a pool of water, where she'd been admiring her reflection. "Oh, thank you!"

"Now, now, just a minute," her fairy godmother cautioned. "You must understand, my dear. At the stroke of twelve the spell will be broken, and everything will be as it was before."

"Oh, I understand," Cinderella said. "But it's more than I ever hoped for."

"Bless you, my child," the fairy godmother said, gently patting the girl on the cheek. It was getting late. She quickly led Cinderella to the carriage. "Hurry up, my dear. The ball can't wait. Have a good time. Dance and be gay. Now, off you go. You're on your way."

Cinderella got into the coach, and the footman closed the door. The young girl waved happily to her fairy godmother. The poor girl had suffered more than her share of woes. The fairy godmother waved back, praying that all her dreams would now come true. A moment later the sparkling carriage sped away into the night, with the promise of a magical evening ahead.

WAXING POETIC

Oh, Cogsworth, have some patience, please
And let me set your mind at ease.
Have you not thought the girl named Belle
Could be the one to break the spell?

We'll serve her all the very best
And make her feel a welcome guest.
We'll put on such a dazzling show,
She just might have some fun, you know.

The objects will all sing and dance—
We'll put her in an utter trance!
We mustn't let her run away
Before she's tasted our soufflé.

If she enjoys our little feast—
Perhaps she'd learn to love the Beast?
To be a human, once again—
Oh, what a feast we will have then!

FIT FOR A PRINCE

Rain splashed down on the stone balcony of the dark castle. The Beast lay on his back, mortally wounded by Gaston's knife. Belle kneeled over him and stroked his wet face.

Slowly the Beast opened his eyes and looked up at her in wonder. "You came back," he whispered.

"Of course I came back." Belle cradled his head in her arms. "I couldn't let them . . ." Overcome with grief, her voice trailed off.

"This is all my fault," she cried, pressing her face to his chest. "If only I'd gotten here sooner."

Neither of them heard the clatter as Cogsworth, Lumiere, and Mrs. Potts ran into the Beast's room. They stopped, frozen with shock at the sight of their master on the wet balcony floor. Behind them, inside the bell jar, the last wilting petal of the enchanted rose wavered.

One cold night many years before, an old beggar woman had come to the castle, offering a rose in exchange for shelter. When the cruel young prince who lived there turned her away, the beggar revealed her true identity. She was a beautiful enchantress, and although the prince begged for her forgiveness, she turned him into a hideous beast, and all the members of his castle staff into household objects. She gave the Beast the rose and said:

"This rose will bloom until your twenty-first birthday, and then it will

wither and die. You have until then to break the spell. If you don't, you will be doomed to remain a beast forever."

Then the enchantress told him that the spell could only be broken by his loving another person and earning that person's love in return.

Now, slumped on the wet balcony, certain that he would soon be dead, the Beast could only mutter, "Maybe . . . maybe it's better this way." For the truth was, he would just as soon die than remain a beast for all eternity.

"Don't talk like that," Belle said in a trembling voice. "You'll be all right. We're together now. Everything's going to be fine, you'll see."

The Beast reached toward her with his massive paw and gently stroked her hair. "At least I got to see you one last time," he whispered.

Belle cradled his paw in her hands, but suddenly she felt it go limp. The Beast's eyes closed again, and his head thudded against the cold, wet stone as he lost consciousness. Belle brought her hands to her mouth to stifle a cry. "No!" she gasped, leaning closer to him. "No! Please! Please don't leave me."

But the Beast lay motionless on the wet floor, and Belle could only bury her face in his chest and sob, "I love you."

At that very moment the last petal of the wilting rose fell from its stem and drifted slowly to the table. Cogsworth, Lumiere, and Mrs. Potts looked down sadly.

Out on the balcony Belle continued to cry. Blinded by her tears, she didn't see the streaks of colorful light that began to fall around them, mixed with the rain. Suddenly she felt an odd sensation and looked up. Drops of glowing rain had begun to collect around the Beast's body. Enshrouded in this misty light, the Beast began to rise magically into the air!

Belle rose and backed away in astonishment. What was happening? How was this possible?

Cogsworth, Lumiere, and Mrs. Potts watched in amazement as the Beast floated in the air above them and slowly turned. Like Belle, they knew something incredible was taking place. Meanwhile, beams of colorful light burst from the Beast's paws. They began to change shape, turning into human hands and feet. More beams flashed as his beastly face was slowly replaced by the face of a young man.

In stunned silence Belle watched the Beast's human form drift gently back to the balcony floor. Completely bewildered by what had happened, she bent forward to touch him, then quickly backed away as he started to stir. The handsome young man slowly stood up. He stared with astonishment at one hand and then the other, then down at his human body. He was no longer a beast but a prince again. Only now there was no trace of the cruel, selfish nature he had shown as a boy.

He spun around and faced Belle. "Belle, it's me!" he gasped, stepping toward her.

Speechless, Belle reached up cautiously and felt his hair. She traced the features of his face with her fingers, then looked into his eyes.

"It . . . it *is* you," she whispered.

The prince gently brushed Belle's wet hair away from her face. They moved closer to each other and closed their eyes for a lingering kiss. As they did, a spiral of magic swirled around them and shot into the sky, exploding like fireworks and bathing the dark, decaying castle in light.

Just as the Beast had been changed back into a handsome prince, the castle was now transformed as well. Its dark, foreboding stone turned bright, and the fierce gargoyles that guarded its turrets became beautiful angels. As Cogsworth, Lumiere, and Mrs. Potts raced happily toward their master, a shower of golden sparkles washed over them. Lumiere spun in the air and once again became the charming maître d' he had been so many years before. Cogsworth found himself back in the robust body of the head of the household, and Mrs. Potts was once again the plump, sweet cook.

"Lumiere!" the prince cried, hugging him. "Cogsworth! Mrs. Potts! Look at us!"

A footstool carrying the little teacup, Chip, ran out onto the balcony and spun around in a flurry of magic. The footstool became a friendly dog, and the teacup a laughing little boy with a chipped tooth.

"It is a miracle!" Lumiere cried.

The prince swept Belle into his arms, and they twirled joyously around the balcony. Their love had broken the spell. This was truly the most enchanted day of their lives.

RAFIKI KNOWS

Oh, lion, trust in this baboon
By the sun and by the moon
You will be a king quite soon

A glob of this, a smear of that
I've got this formula down pat
I know just where you're hiding at

And when you turn your gaze up high
You'll see your father in the sky
Then you'll understand just why

An old baboon like me is key
To make you realize and see
A king is what you're meant to be.

A STARRY NIGHT

Rafiki, the great mystic, stood on the broad, grassy plain under the clear African sky. He sensed something in the air. A sudden breeze carried a wispy puff of milkweed seeds toward him, and the wise baboon reached up and caught it.

Interesting, Rafiki thought as he scrambled back to his hollow tree. There he tossed the seeds into an old tortoiseshell and added the sticky contents of a gourd. He mixed them well and then moved to a crude drawing of a young lion cub on the trunk of the tree. It was a picture of Simba, the lion prince who had vanished many years before on the day his father, the great lion king Mufasa, died.

Rafiki took a handful of the milkweed mixture and spread it around the head and shoulders of the cub in the drawing. Now the drawing showed a full-grown lion with a beautiful mane.

The spirited old baboon couldn't help smiling. It was just as he had always suspected: Simba was alive!

A few nights later Rafiki sat in a tree near a stream and waited. The night sky was filled with glittering stars and lit by the moon. Soon a handsome lion stepped into the clearing.

Ah, Simba, Rafiki thought, it's good to see you again after so many years. You walk with your father's dignity. He will be proud.

Simba stopped beside the stream and gazed down forlornly at his reflection.

"I'm no king," the young lion said in a sad, defeated voice. "I can't go back." He shook his head. "I'm not you, Dad. I'll never be you."

"Asante sana. Squash banana," the old baboon began to sing to the young lion whom he had blessed as a cub many years before. *"We we nugu. Mi mi apana."*

Simba looked around, then squinted up into the tree where Rafiki sat. Not seeing anyone, he walked along the stream.

When Simba stopped to rest on a fallen log above the stream, Rafiki threw a stone into the water near him. As the water rippled away, the old baboon again sang, *"Asante sana. Squash banana. We we nugu. Mi mi apana."*

"Cut it out," Simba snapped, eyeing Rafiki. Simba rose and started away, but Rafiki followed. Finally the young lion turned and said, "Would you stop following me?"

But Rafiki had no intention of stopping.

"Who are you?" Simba asked.

"The question is," Rafiki replied, stepping closer, "who are *you*?"

Simba sighed. "I thought I knew. Now I'm not so sure."

"I know who you are," Rafiki said. "You're Mufasa's boy."

The old baboon watched Simba's eyes widen in shock. Now that he had the young lion's attention, it was time to scoot away through the underbrush.

"Wait!" Simba cried, crashing through the brush behind him.

Rafiki raced up to the top of a small hill and then sat down and crossed his legs. A moment later Simba arrived, huffing and puffing to catch his breath.

"You knew my father?" he gasped.

"Correction," replied Rafiki. "I *know* your father."

"I hate to tell you this," Simba said, still panting, "but my father died a long time ago."

"Nope, wrong again," Rafiki replied, getting up. "Your father's alive. I'll show him to you. You follow old Rafiki. He knows the way."

Rafiki moved off quickly into the dark, dense jungle on the other side of the hill. "Hurry up!" he shouted back to Simba. "Don't dawdle! Mufasa's waiting!"

The young lion bounded into the jungle after Rafiki. "Hey, wait! Hold up! Where are you going?"

The baboon kept running until he saw some reeds ahead. Suddenly he spun around and held up his hand. "Stop!"

Simba stopped. Rafiki turned to the reeds and parted them, revealing a dark pool of still water. "Look down there."

"Why?"

"Just look!" Rafiki urged him. "Do you see Mufasa?"

The young lion looked down at the mirrorlike surface. "That's not my father. It's just my reflection."

"Look *harder*," Rafiki exhorted.

He and Simba stared down at the reflection. Gradually Simba's image changed into a vision of Mufasa.

"You see?" Rafiki said with a smile. "He lives in you."

"*Simba. . . ,*" the reflection spoke.

Simba was so startled, he began to back away, but Rafiki put a reassuring hand on his shoulder and stopped him.

"Father?" Simba gasped, amazed, as the ghostly reflection began to materialize in the night sky.

"*Simba, have you forgotten me?*" Mufasa's ghost asked.

"No!" Simba cried. "How could I?"

"You have forgotten who you are," the ghostly image said. "And so you have forgotten me."

Simba stared up at the vision growing larger in the sky.

"Look inside yourself, Simba," Mufasa said. "You are more than what you have become. You must take your place in the Circle of Life."

"But I've made a place for myself here," Simba said. "I'm not who I used to be. How can I go back?"

"Remember who you are," Mufasa said. "You are my son and the one true king."

The ghost began to disappear. "Remember who you are. . . ." The voice began to fade.

"No! Please!" Simba cried. "Don't leave me!"

"Remember . . ." Mufasa's voice was distant now.

"Father?" Simba called desperately.

"Remember. . . ," the voice said one last time, and then vanished.

Simba stepped back from the reeds, and Rafiki let them close. The young lion's eyes met the old baboon's, and Rafiki could see that something had changed. Rafiki watched with a smile on his face. He knew that Simba would return to Pride Rock to claim his position as king. Like his father before him, Simba would now take his place in the Circle of Life.

WOULDN'T YOU LIKE TO FLY?

You children down there—do you want to fly?
To be just like me and take to the sky?
Or stay safe in your beds. Ha! What a pity!
When you could fly with me past the roofs of the city!

If you come with me, I might give you a look
At dangerous pirates and cruel Captain Hook.
Never Land's only a short trip away—
If we take off right now, we can get there today!

Come, Wendy, come, Michael, come, John, if you trust,
Now where is old Tink with a dash of that dust?
Just think happy thoughts and soon you'll be reeling
As you easily float from the floor to the ceiling!

PIXIE DUST AND HAPPY THOUGHTS

It was Tinker Bell who finally found Peter Pan's shadow in the Darling children's nursery. Peter quickly opened the dresser drawer, and sure enough, out flew his shadow. Now he sat on Wendy's bed, playing his panpipes, while she sewed his shadow back on.

"How in the world did you lose your shadow?" Wendy asked.

Peter explained that Nana, the Darling family's dog, had stolen his shadow several nights earlier while he was at the window.

"What were you doing there?" Wendy asked as she sewed.

"I came to listen to the stories," Peter explained.

"*My* stories?" Wendy said, surprised. "But they're all about you!"

"Of course," Peter said. "That's why I like them. I tell them to the Lost Boys."

Wendy sewed the last stitch in place. "Oh, yes, the Lost Boys who live with you in Never Land."

"That's right." Peter hopped off the bed and studied his shadow against the wall. Wendy had sewn it on quite tightly, and it wasn't about to get away again.

"I'm so glad you came back tonight," Wendy said with a sigh. "I might never have seen you."

"Why?" asked Peter, who was still admiring his shadow.

"Because I have to grow up tomorrow," Wendy said.

Peter spun around, shocked. "Grow up?"

Wendy nodded sadly. "Tonight's my last night in the nursery."

"But that means no more stories," Peter said.

"I know," Wendy said with a sniff.

"No, I won't have it!" Peter grabbed her hand and led her across the room. "Come on!"

"Where are we going?" Wendy asked, startled.

"To Never Land." Peter started to pull her toward the open window. "You'll never grow up there."

"Oh, Peter, that would be wonderful!" Wendy gasped. But before he could pull her out the window, she stopped. "Wait! What would Mother say?"

"Mother?" Peter scowled as he floated in the air. "What's a mother?"

Wendy stared up at him, awestruck that he could float so effortlessly in the air.

"Well . . . a mother's someone who loves you and cares for you and tells you stories," she explained.

"Good." Peter grabbed Wendy's hand again. "You'll be our mother."

"Now just a minute." Wendy backed away. "I have to pack and leave a note where I'll be. Of course, I couldn't stay too long, but—" She suddenly stopped. "Never Land! I'm so happy, I think I'll give you a kiss."

Trapped inside the dresser drawer all this time, Tinker Bell had grown more and more jealous. Peter was so busy listening to Wendy, he didn't even realize that Tinker Bell was stuck. The thought of that talkative girl kissing Peter made Tinker Bell redouble her efforts to escape. With all her might she forced the drawer open and burst into the air.

Across the room, Peter nervously backed away from Wendy. "What's a kiss?"

"I'll show you," Wendy said. She pursed her lips and stepped toward him. Without warning, something yanked her back by the hair.

76

"Ouch!" Wendy cried.

"Stop it, Tink!" Peter started chasing the pixie around the room, waking Wendy's brother Michael in the process.

When Michael saw Peter, he cried out for his brother. "John! John, wake up! He's here!"

A sleepy-looking John sat up, put on his glasses, and saw Peter catch Tinker Bell in his hat and return to Wendy's side.

"What in the world was that?" Wendy asked, smoothing her hair.

"Tinker Bell," Peter said, opening his hat to show her. "I don't know what's gotten into her."

Michael and John jumped out of bed and joined them. The boys gazed with wonder at the tiny blond fairy.

"Look," said Michael, "a firefly!"

"A pixie," Wendy guessed.

Tinker Bell sat inside Peter's hat and twinkled angrily, creating a tiny shower of glitter.

"What's the pixie doing?" Michael asked.

"Talking," Peter replied.

"What did she say?" asked Wendy.

"She says you're a big ugly girl." Peter laughed as Tinker Bell flew out of the hat and alighted on a bookcase.

Wendy held her chin high. "Well, I think *she's* lovely."

Peter pointed toward the open window. "Come on, Wendy, let's go."

"Where are we going?" Michael asked.

"To Never Land," Wendy answered. "Peter's taking us."

"Us?" Peter scowled.

"I couldn't go without Michael and John," Wendy told him.

"I should like very much to cross swords with some real buccaneers," John said eagerly.

"And fight pirates, too," Michael added.

Peter smiled. "All right, but you have to take orders."

"Aye, aye, sir!" John saluted.

"Me, too," said Michael.

"But how do we get to Never Land?" Wendy asked.

"We fly," Peter said matter-of-factly.

"*Fly?*" Wendy looked puzzled. "But how?"

"It's easy. All you have to do is . . ." Peter paused and rubbed his chin. "That's funny."

"What's the matter?" asked Wendy. "Don't you know how?"

"Sure," Peter said. "It's just that I never thought about it before." After a moment, his eyes lit up. "That's it! You have to think of a wonderful thought."

"Any happy little thought?" John and Wendy asked.

"Uh-huh." Peter nodded.

"Like toys at Christmas?" asked Wendy.

"And sleigh bells and snow?" John added.

"Yes. Now watch. Here I go!" Peter rose toward the ceiling. "Now you try."

"I'll think of a mermaid lagoon under a magic moon," said Wendy.

"I'll think I'm in a pirate's cave," said John.

"I'll be an Indian brave!" cried Michael.

Everyone held hands as Peter pulled them up into the air and then let go. Wendy and the boys floated for a moment near the ceiling but suddenly tumbled down and landed with a crash on the bed. Tinker Bell laughed while Peter hovered in the air above them and frowned.

"What's the matter?" he said. "All it takes is a little faith and trust. . . . Oh, there's something I forgot—dust!"

Wendy and John frowned. "Dust?"

Tinker Bell knew what Peter was referring to, so she quickly darted away. But Peter caught the little fairy and shook her over the Darling children. Sparkling pixie dust fell around them like a fine powdery snow.

"Now think of the happiest things," Peter instructed them. "It's the same as having wings."

"Let's all try it once more," Wendy said. Suddenly she and her brothers began to float.

"Look!" John cried in amazement. "We're rising off the floor!"

"I don't believe it!" Wendy gasped.

"We can fly!" they shouted with delight.

The next thing they knew, they were drifting up near the ceiling again, only this time they stayed there. Peter stood by the window and watched them circle the chandelier. "Come on, everybody!" he called. "Here we go to Never Land!" He jumped out the window, and the others followed. Michael brought his teddy bear, and John wore a top hat and carried an umbrella. The night air was cool as they flew over the rooftops of London, past Big Ben, then up through the cloudy skies toward the second star, and straight on till morning . . . to the mysterious place called Never Land.